The BEARS FIND THANKSGIVING

Story by
John Barrett

Illustrations by
Rick Reinert Productions

Developed by
The LeFave Company

CHILDRENS PRESS, CHICAGO

School & Library Edition

Copyright © MCMLXXXI by The LeFave Company
All rights reserved. Printed and bound in U.S.A.
Published simultaneously in Canada.

New ISBN 0-516-09192-1

Former ISBN 0-8249-8019-0

The bears of
Bearbank were
getting ready for
the famous
Thanksgiving Day
Honey Bowl Parade
and football game.

Ted Edward Bear—Ted E. Bear for short—said to his friends, "We should build a float for the Honey Bowl Parade!"

Henry Bear laughed, "Only big businesses build floats for the Honey Bowl Parade."

Patti Bear shook her head. "Building a parade float costs a lot of money," she said.

$\mathcal{T}$ed E. Bear went to the parade office.

C. Emory Bear was the Grand Marshall of the parade. He growled, "You can't have a float in the Honey Bowl Parade! It is a big, important parade. You are just a little bear. Your float wouldn't be good enough!"

$\mathcal{T}$eddy returned with the sad news.

"I told you so," said Patti Bear.

"Well, I'm going to build a float for Thanksgiving anyway," Ted brightened. "When the Grand Marshall sees how good it is, he will surely change his mind."

"What will you put on your float?" asked Henry.

Teddy was puzzled. He hadn't thought about decorating his float.

"I'll go ask Bum Bear," he said. "He's very smart. Maybe he can tell me what Thanksgiving is all about."

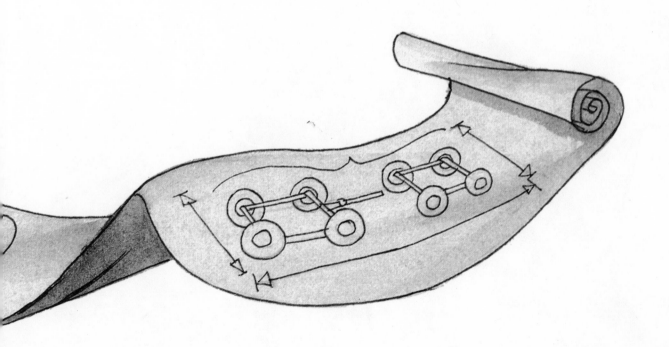

"When the first bears came to this country, they didn't have fine clothes and big houses. But every year, they gave thanks for all the things they did have," Bum Bear explained. "They called the holiday **Thanksgiving.**"

Bum Bear sighed, "It was a wonderful holiday. Every year bear families would gather together, cook a big turkey, and spend the day giving thanks."

"Why did bears stop giving thanks?" asked Ted E. Bear.

"With all the excitement of the Honey Bowl, they probably just forgot," said Bum Bear.

"Bears can be thankful for so many things," said Teddy. "I will build a float that will remind them."

He took the wheels from his wagon. He found some old boards. He pasted paper on the boards. Then he built a huge horn of plenty and set it on the float. Inside he placed a table. Finally, Ted and his friends cooked a huge turkey to set on the table.

On the day of the parade, Patti and Henry helped Teddy push the float to Bearbank Boulevard.

"I'm sure the Grand Marshall will think our float is good," said Ted E. Bear. "We might even win first prize!"

"I don't know about that," said Patti Bear.

"No!" shouted the Grand Marshall. "I won't allow that little, homemade float in my parade. This is the Honey Bowl, not the Turkey Bowl!"

"I knew it," sighed Patti Bear.

Sadly, Teddy and his friends pushed
their Thanksgiving float up a small hill, out
of the way of the parade.

$\mathcal{A}$ whistle blew! The parade began! The Grizzly University Marching Band played the Bearbank marching song.

The Grizzly Cowbear Cheerleaders
danced in perfect step.

The crowd cheered.

The Bearbank Power and Light Company's
float was fantastic!

The bears along the street cheered.

The Bear National Bank's float was beautiful!
It showed what a wealthy town Bearbank was.

The crowd was thrilled.

*B*ear Air—the airline of the bears—entered a huge float. It showed the bears' conquest of the sky and space.

The crowd applauded.

The Organic Honeyworks' float showed
the bears' huge supply of honey.

The parade was almost over. Teddy, Patti and Henry were disappointed. "It's too bad," said Teddy. "Not one of the floats said anything about giving thanks."

The three began to push the little float home. But the float began to roll down the hill instead.

"Stop it!" shouted Teddy.

"I can't!" yelled Henry.

"Oh no!" said Patti. "We're going to be in the parade after all!"

The little float bumped into the last float and rolled behind it in the big parade.

$\mathcal{T}$he crowd stopped cheering. The judges were puzzled. "How did this little float get into the Honey Bowl Parade?" everyone asked.

Then a hush fell over the crowd. The bears realized they had forgotten the most important part of Thanksgiving—giving thanks.

At the half time ceremony in Honey Bowl Stadium, the judges announced the winning parade float:

"All the floats were beautiful. They showed us all the fine things we bears have. But one float was very special. It reminded us of something we almost forgot—that bears should be **thankful** for all those wonderful things.

"The first prize in this year's Honey Bowl Parade goes to Ted E. Bear!"

The crowd clapped and cheered. They were very thankful bears.

And so was Ted E. Bear!